WS

RA

Please return/renew this item by the last date shown

worcestershire
countycouncil
Libraries & Learning

Russell Pun...
Illustrated by
Gustavo Ma...

D0265052

This story is about
an old woman,

an old
man,

an
enormous
peach,

2

a brave little boy,

a dog,

a monkey

and a pheasant.

3

Once upon a time, an old
man and an old woman
lived by a river.

Every Monday, the old
woman went to the river
to wash their clothes.

One morning, she saw
something floating on
the water.

It was the biggest peach
she had ever seen.

She fished out the peach
and rolled it home.

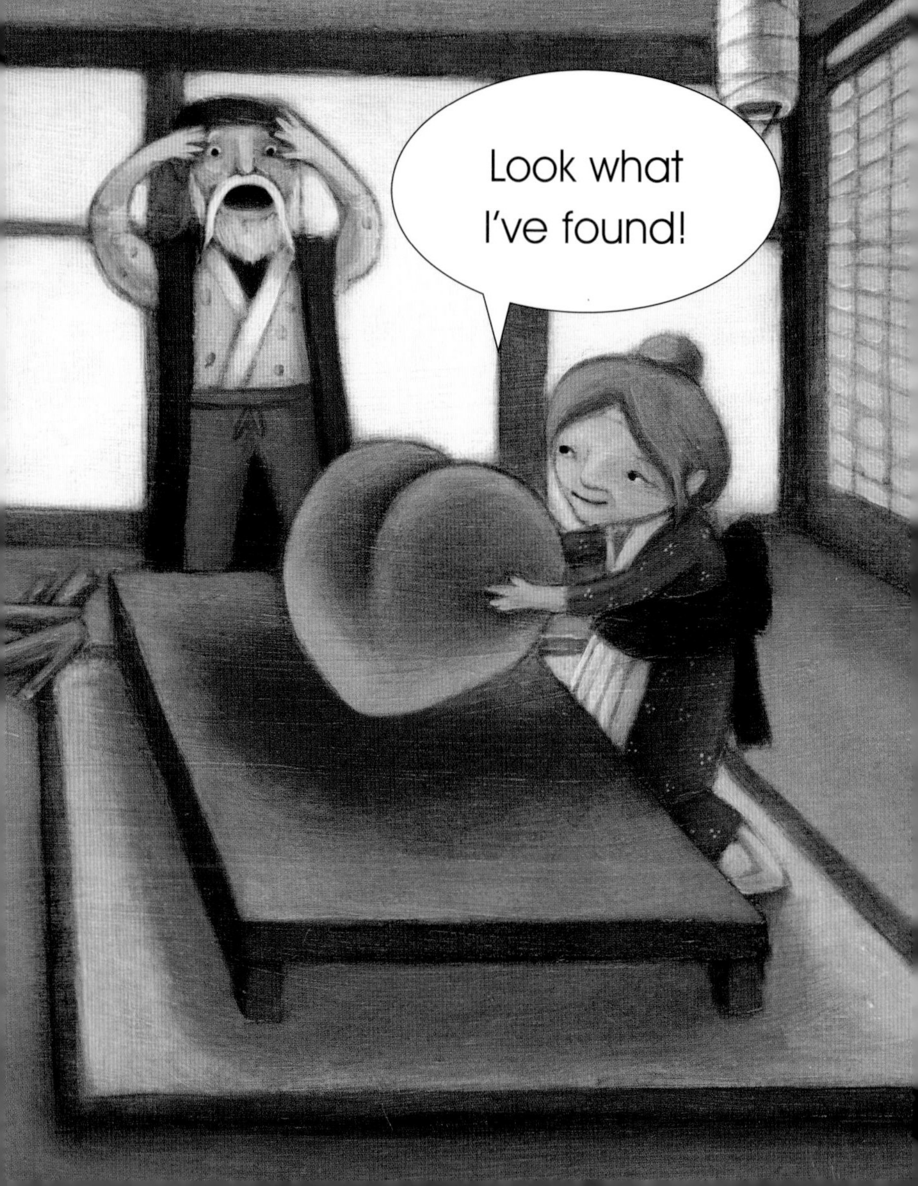

"It looks very juicy. Let's eat it!" said the old man.

And he started to cut it open.

Suddenly, the peach
split in two.

Inside, there was a
little boy!

10

"What a lovely child,"
said the old woman. "Let's
call him Peach Boy."

"He can be our son."

Peach Boy grew up
quickly.

Soon, he was the strongest,
fastest boy in the village.

He was also a champion
fighter with his
wooden sword.

One day, Peach Boy came
to a nearby village.

What's
happened?

The people in the
village were very upset.

14

"Giant ogres came and took all our jewels," they cried.

"Don't worry," said Peach Boy. "I'll get them back."

"Where do the ogres live?"

"They came from Ogre Island," said a villager. "It's in the West."

Peach Boy's parents didn't
want him to go.

But Peach Boy had
made up his mind.

18

So his father gave Peach
Boy his finest sword.

And his mother gave him
six dumplings to eat on
the way.

At last, Peach
Boy set off for
Ogre Island.

21

He hadn't gone far,
when he met a dog.

"I've heard about you,
Peach Boy," said Dog.

"Give me a dumpling
and I'll help you fight
the ogres."

"Alright," said Peach
Boy, and he threw Dog
a dumpling.

The
next day,
Peach Boy and Dog
came to a dark forest.

"I can smell something in that tree," said Dog.

"Show yourself!" shouted Peach Boy. He wasn't afraid of anything.

A monkey jumped
out of the tree and
landed in front of them.

27

"Are you Peach Boy?"
asked Monkey.

"Yes he is," growled Dog, "and he doesn't need your help."

"Be quiet Dog," said Peach Boy. And he gave Monkey a dumpling.

A day
later, the
three were
climbing up
a steep hill.

"I can smell something
behind that rock,"
said Dog.

"I can see feathers,"
said Monkey.

A pheasant hopped onto
the rock.

SQUAWK!
Hello, Peach
Boy.

"If you give me a
dumpling, I'll help you."

"We don't need your help,"
said Dog and Monkey
together.

"Shh!" said Peach Boy.

And he gave Pheasant
a dumpling.

Finally,
they came to
the top of the
hill. Through
the mist, they
could all see
Ogre Island.

"How will we get there?" asked Dog.

"I'll build a boat," said Peach Boy.

36

Peach Boy was the captain.
Dog and Monkey rowed
the boat.

Pheasant flew ahead to
look for ogres.

Soon they landed on
Ogre Island.

38

"The Ogre King and his ogres are inside the castle," Pheasant called. "They're having a feast."

The giant ogres didn't hear Peach Boy, Dog and Monkey creep into the castle.

A fierce battle broke out.
Dog bit the ogres' ankles.

Ouch!

Pheasant pecked at their
hands and heads.

And Monkey jumped on
their backs.

Get off!
Get off!

But Peach Boy went
straight to the Ogre King.

"I'm not scared of you!"
roared the Ogre King.

"You should be," said
Peach Boy.

44

He jumped onto the blade
of the Ogre King's sword.
"Say sorry!"

"Sorry," huffed the Ogre King.

"Promise you'll never attack anyone again," said Peach Boy.

Do I have to?

Yes!

"I promise," he agreed.